SOCCER 'CATS

Matt Christopher®

Heads Up

Text by Stephanie Peters

Illustrated by Daniel Vasconcellos

LITTLE, BROWN AND COMPANY

New York ⌇ An AOL Time Warner Company

*To my great-granddaughter
Tiffany Marie Howell*

Text copyright © 2000 by Catherine M. Christopher
Illustrations copyright © 2000 by Daniel Vasconcellos

First Paperback Edition

Library of Congress Cataloging-in-Publication Data

Peters, Stephanie.
    Heads Up / [by Matt Christopher] ; text by Stephanie Peters; illustrated by Daniel Vasconcellos.—1st ed.
        p.   cm.—(Soccer Cats ; #6)
    Summary: After a hit to the face that knocks her out momentarily, a soccer halfback develops a fear of the ball.
    ISBN 0-316-13504-6 (hc)/ISBN 0-316-16497-6 (pb)
    [1. Soccer—Fiction.] I. Vasconcellos, Daniel, ill. II. Title.

PZ7.P441835 He   2001
[Fic]—dc21   00-041229

HC: 10 9 8 7 6 5 4 3 2 1
PB: 10 9 8 7 6 5 4 3 2 1

WOR (hc)

COM-MO (pb)

Printed in the United States of America

Soccer 'Cats Team Roster

Lou Barnes	*Striker*
Jerry Dinh	*Striker*
Stookie Norris	*Striker*
Dewey London	*Halfback*
Bundy Neel	*Halfback*
Amanda Caler	*Halfback*
Brant Davis	*Fullback*
Lisa Gaddy	*Fullback*
Ted Gaddy	*Fullback*
Alan Minter	*Fullback*
Bucky Pinter	*Goalie*

Subs:

Jason Shearer

Dale Tuget

Roy Boswick

Edith "Eddie" Sweeny

Chapter 1

"**H**ere!" a familiar voice yelled from Amanda Caler's right side.

Amanda, left halfback for the Soccer 'Cats soccer team, glanced up to see Stookie Norris waving to her. He was in the clear so she kicked the ball to him. It was a perfect shot to the striker. Stookie stopped the ball, dribbled half a dozen feet toward the goal, then gave it a hard kick at the net.

Goal!

"Good shot, Stookie!" several 'Cats yelled.

The fans yelled, too. The score narrowed the gap. Now instead of Panthers 3, 'Cats 0, it was Panthers 3, 'Cats 1.

But the game was in its final minutes and the chances of the 'Cats scoring again were slim. That dismal thought raced through Amanda's mind as she watched the Panthers move the ball down the field with short, sure-footed passes.

The ball crossed the center line before Amanda could reach it. Three Panthers were passing the ball among them, eluding their attackers like mice eluding cats.

For a couple of seconds Amanda studied their pattern. When she sensed an oppor-tunity to steal the ball, she raced in. With a lightning-quick move, she trapped the ball with the instep of her right foot, spun, and dribbled the ball out of the attacking zone.

The Panthers were caught by surprise. That gave Amanda enough time to move the ball deeper into the Panthers' territory. Jerry Dinh came up alongside her, but Amanda kept control of the ball until she saw an attacker sweeping up from her other side.

"Jerry!" she called and passed the ball to him.

Jerry, a striker, slowed it down with the instep of his foot. Two Panthers were on him in an instant.

Amanda followed, ready to receive a pass if Jerry got into trouble.

Jerry did get in trouble. Usually as cool as a cucumber, he looked flustered as both Panthers stabbed at the ball with their feet.

Stookie Norris swooped in to try to help, but the Panthers boxed him out. "Get rid of it!" Stookie cried.

Jerry didn't hesitate. He walloped the ball as hard as he could—right at Amanda.

Blam! Amanda was hit full force in the face! The contact was so solid, she saw stars.

Then she saw something else. Blood, and lots of it. It was spilling from her nose onto her shirt. One look was all she got. Dizziness swept over her. The last thing she remembered was hitting the turf.

Chapter 2

When Amanda came to, she found herself being carried. Something cold was pressed against her nose.

"Hey, what's going on?" she cried, struggling to get free.

"Whoa, hold on a minute," came a deep voice. It was Coach Bradley, the person who was carrying her. He removed the ice pack from her nose and sat her down gently on the bench.

"Are you okay?" he asked, looking at her

with concern. "That was some nosebleed you got."

She touched her nose gingerly. The bleeding had stopped. "Guess I passed out," she mumbled.

The coach smiled. "Guess you did. Are you in much pain?"

She wiggled her nose from side to side. "No, it's not too bad," she said. "I think I can keep playing."

The coach shook his head. "I don't think so. You're sitting out the rest of the game, Amanda." He pulled a cell phone out of his team duffel bag. "In fact, I'm calling your mother to come get you right now."

Amanda's heart sank. Her mother turned white at the sight of a skinned knee. She usually stayed away from Amanda's soccer games because she didn't want to see anyone get hurt. What would she do when she heard Amanda had had a bloody nose?

And what about her T-shirt? There was enough blood on it to equal a dozen skinned knees!

Well, she couldn't stop the coach from calling her mom. But maybe he could help with the T-shirt.

"Uh, Coach, do you have any extra Soccer 'Cats shirts in that bag? I think mine is ruined."

Coach Bradley nodded. "Go ahead and look. You can change in the rest room."

Amanda searched the bag and found what she was looking for. As she started toward the bathroom, Coach Bradley called, "Take Eddie with you, just in case."

Edith "Eddie" Sweeny looked up, surprised. But she slid off the bench and joined Amanda.

"What does he think is going to happen to you?" Eddie grumbled, shaking her head of fiery red hair. "Now I'll miss the end of the game. Not that I was going to get in again anyway. He always subs Dale in for you instead of me. I don't know why. I think I'd make a pretty good halfback, don't you?"

Amanda didn't know what to say. Eddie was a good player, but she was hot-tempered sometimes. That could come in handy on defense, when the team needed someone to battle hard for possession of the ball. But on offense, one needed a cool head. A big part of the halfback's job was helping set up offensive plays. Amanda wasn't sure Eddie would be any good at that.

So instead of answering, Amanda ducked into a bathroom stall and pulled off her old shirt. As she struggled into the new shirt, she said, "We better hurry and get back to the team to shake hands."

When Amanda emerged from the bathroom holding the old shirt, Eddie was frowning. She looked like she was about to say something, but didn't. Instead, she looked at the shirt in Amanda's hand.

"Boy, I bet it hurt when you got hit," she said finally. "Sure hope it doesn't make you afraid of the ball."

Chapter 3

The girls walked back to the bench in silence. Amanda felt guilty for not having answered Eddie's question.

But then again, she told herself, *my mother always says if you can't say something nice, then don't say anything at all.*

Amanda's mother arrived shortly after the girls returned. As Amanda expected, her mother looked like she was about to faint.

"Oh, my poor little girl," she cried as she crushed Amanda in a bear hug. "I knew this

game was dangerous. Why, oh why, won't you take up ballet like your sister?"

Amanda rolled her eyes. "Because I don't like wearing tights and toe shoes, Mom. I like wearing shorts and sneakers. Now let go, you're squeezing the stuffing out of me!"

"The coach said you collapsed on the field!"

"I fainted when I saw the blood," Amanda admitted and instantly wished that she hadn't.

"Blood! What blood? Oh, my, there was blood?" Mrs. Caler was getting more and more upset.

Coach Bradley stepped in.

"Now, now, Amanda's fine. She took a hit in the nose, so naturally she got a nosebleed. But the nose stopped bleeding right away, and she's been perfectly fine ever since. Right, Amanda?"

Mrs. Caler looked from her daughter to the coach and back again. She seemed to be calming down. Then Eddie stepped forward.

14

"Here, Amanda, don't forget your old shirt. Though I don't guess you'll be wanting to wear it again on account of how it looks." She shook the shirt out right under Mrs. Caler's nose.

Mrs. Caler took one look, made a strangled noise in the back of her throat, and crumpled to the ground.

"What did you do that for?" Amanda yelled, rushing forward to her mother. She patted her mother's face gently, like she'd seen people do in movies.

Eddie widened her eyes. "Gee, sorry. Boy, talk about 'like mother, like daughter'! She passed out even quicker than you did when you saw the blood!"

When Mrs. Caler came to, Coach Bradley insisted on driving her and Amanda home. "Your husband can come back for your car later," he said when Mrs. Caler tried to protest. "Besides, it will give me a chance to convince you that soccer is just as safe as ballet."

"Hmph," sniffed Mrs. Caler. She waved a hand at the bloody T-shirt Eddie was still holding. "You'll never find a ballerina wearing something like that!" She wobbled unsteadily to the car.

Eddie came alongside Amanda. "Your mom seems pretty upset. You don't think she'd make you quit the team, do you?"

Amanda looked at Eddie with surprise. "No, she wouldn't do that. I mean, it was only one little nosebleed, after all."

Eddie gazed after Mrs. Caler. "Right. One little nosebleed wouldn't be enough." She tossed Amanda's old T-shirt into the trash can and dusted her hands clean. "Well, see you at practice tomorrow!"

Chapter 4

The next day shone bright and clear, perfect for playing soccer. Amanda was looking forward to practice from the moment she got out of bed.

An hour after breakfast she hurried to join her teammates.

"Hi, Amanda," Jason Shearer said, popping his gum. "Didn't think we'd see you here today."

"Why not?" Amanda replied.

"Oh, I don't . . . don't . . . know—ooh, oooh!" Jason pretended to faint.

Amanda made a face. "Very funny," she said. She balled her hand up into a fist and waved it under Jason's nose. "Maybe I should show you up close and personal what it's like to get a bloody nose."

"All right, that's enough," said Bundy Neel, captain of the Soccer 'Cats. "Jason, don't you ever stop clowning around?"

"Only when I'm in the goal!" Jason danced away.

Bundy turned to Amanda. "Seriously, how are you feeling today?"

Amanda shrugged. "Fine," she said.

But suddenly she wasn't so sure. Jason's little joke had reminded her of how painful being hit had been. And fainting hadn't been any picnic either, if the truth were to be told.

But getting hit was a fluke, a one-time thing, she tried to reassure herself. *The odds against it happening again are a million to one.*

Coach Bradley appeared a minute later.

The 'Cats did their usual warm-up drills, then the coach called them together.

"I had a call last night asking if we could practice heading the ball today," he announced. "So unless there are any objections, let's start the drill."

No one said anything, though they glanced at each other. Amanda could guess what they were thinking, because she was thinking the same thing: Who had made the call to the coach? No one seemed to know.

Just then, Eddie appeared.

"Sorry I'm late!" was all she said.

The coach nodded, then organized the drill.

"Count off A-B, A-B." The 'Cats did. "Okay, I want the A players on the center line. Spread out so there's plenty of room between you."

The A's moved to the center line.

"Now the B's form a line about five feet away from them." Amanda joined the rest of the B's. The coach started rolling a soccer ball to each of the A's and explained the rest of the drill.

"The B's are going to kneel down. The A's are going to lob the balls to the B's and the B's are going to head them back as best they can. Kneeling down teaches you not to lunge or jump for the ball. Lunging and jumping could lead to injury."

He rolled the last of the balls to the A's. "Use the part of your forehead that's closest to your hairline. Heading with the top of your head can hurt—and yesterday we saw what happens when you head with your face," he added with a smile.

Amanda knew the coach hadn't meant to embarrass her, yet she reddened anyway as she knelt down. Then she looked up to see who her partner was, and suddenly she was no longer embarrassed. Instead, for a reason she couldn't explain, she was uneasy.

Maybe it was the way Eddie was tossing the ball from hand to hand and grinning.

Chapter 5

"**A**ll set, partner?" Eddie asked.

Amanda gulped, then nodded.

"Well, then, here it comes." Eddie tossed the ball high into the air. So high that Amanda lost sight of it in the sun. She squinted, then suddenly there it was.

She couldn't help herself. She gave a sharp cry, covered her head with her arms, and ducked.

"Whoa!" Coach Bradley hurried up to them. "Everything okay here?"

Amanda was about to answer but Eddie cut

her off. "I don't know what happened, Coach. It's like Amanda's afraid of the ball or something."

Amanda's jaw dropped. "I am not!" she sputtered. "It's just—just—" She was so surprised at Eddie that she couldn't get the words out.

Coach Bradley patted her shoulder. "It's okay, Amanda. It's natural to be afraid after getting hit. Just try not to flinch. Once you've headed the ball successfully a few times, you'll be back in control." He walked away to watch another pair.

Amanda turned to glare at Eddie. "What did you say that for?" she demanded.

"The coach asked a question. When someone asks a question, I answer it."

Amanda looked closely at Eddie, trying to figure out if there was a hidden message in her reply. Like, *I asked you a question in the rest room yesterday and I'm still waiting for my answer.* Amanda couldn't be sure.

With a sigh, she got back into the kneeling position. "Okay, let's do this again. And this time, could you toss it up a little lower?"

Eddie ran a hand through her hair. "Sure, whatever you say," she said.

But it didn't seem to matter how Eddie tossed the ball. Whenever it came close to her head, Amanda shrank back. Only twice did she make good contact.

Eddie, on the other hand, headed the ball with gusto. "Nice job," commented the coach as he watched her send the ball rocketing back into the air. Eddie beamed.

Amanda was relieved when the coach blew the whistle, ending the drill.

Now maybe we'll get to scrimmage, she thought. *And I'll be able to get back into the swing of things!*

Instead, to her dismay, the coach called, "On your feet! It's time to practice heading the ball from the standing position. After all, you'll be standing during the game!"

"Well, the players on the field will be, anyway," joked Jason, who usually started the games sitting on the bench.

"Most of them will be, at least," Eddie added. And she winked at Amanda.

Chapter 6

The rest of practice was a disaster for Amanda. Nearly every time the ball came toward her, she flashed back to the day before and flinched. The few times the ball did make contact with her head hurt. When the drill ended, she felt frustrated.

"Don't worry, you'll get the hang of it," the coach reassured her. But Amanda wasn't so sure. She was happy when the coach called for a scrimmage.

At last! she thought. *Now I can get into the groove.*

But she didn't. It seemed like the other players were eager to try out their new heading skills in a game-like situation. The ball was constantly in the air instead of on the ground — and Amanda felt like a sitting duck waiting to be picked off.

Coach Bradley finally ended the practice. Before everyone left, he reminded the team of the next day's game against the Torpedoes.

Amanda couldn't wait to get home. All she wanted to do was lie in the hammock in her backyard and forget about soccer for the afternoon.

When she pushed open the kitchen door, she found the mail lying on the floor under the mail slot. She picked it up. Along with the usual junk mail and bills was a plain envelope addressed to her mother. The envelope wasn't sealed, and when she tossed it on the counter with the other mail, a piece of paper came fluttering out.

Amanda stooped to retrieve the paper. It

was a newspaper clipping. The headline read:
IS YOUR SOCCER PLAYER SAFE?

Amanda was dumbfounded. She grabbed the envelope and turned it over and over, looking for a sign of who had sent it. She found nothing.

She hesitated. She was burning to know who had sent the clipping. But her mother had always told her not to read other people's mail. Still, if the envelope was already open . . . ?

The sound of a car door slamming solved the problem for her. Hastily, she stuffed the clipping back into the envelope, put the envelope on the counter, and rushed out of the kitchen.

Amanda waited all day for her mother to comment about the envelope. But she didn't. Amanda almost asked her about it. But her mother might think it was odd if she did. After all, Amanda had never asked her about her mail before.

Then, at dinner, she thought she was going to hear about it at last.

"I got something interesting in the mail today," Mrs. Caler said.

"What was it?" Amanda's sister Amelia asked. Amelia was three years older than Amanda. She had just come home from ballet class. As usual, her hair was pulled back into a ponytail and she was wearing a leotard and a pair of shorts.

Amanda held her breath. Was she about to learn what else was in the envelope and who had sent it?

She wasn't. Instead of the plain envelope, Mrs. Caler pulled out a fancy pink one. She waved it at Amelia.

"We finally got that information about ballet school!" she crowed happily. She pulled a booklet out of the envelope and opened it between Amelia and Amanda.

"Doesn't this look wonderful?" she asked the girls.

Amelia's reply was a squeal of delight. Amanda didn't say anything.

After all, her mother had always told her it was better to say nothing at all if you couldn't say something nice.

Chapter 7

Mrs. Caler and Amelia talked about ballet and the ballet school for the rest of the meal. Amanda finished her dinner in silence, cleared her dishes from the table, and went to her room.

Who would have sent Mom that envelope? she asked herself for the thousandth time that day.

She flopped onto her bed and pondered for a while. Suddenly, she sat up.

"Eddie," she said out loud.

Eddie wanted to play halfback. But the

'Cats already had their starting halfbacks—Amanda, Bundy, and Dewey. And Dale was the usual halfback sub. Eddie would only be subbed in at halfback if one of the other four couldn't play.

Amanda couldn't think of any reason why Dewey, Bundy, or Dale wouldn't be able to play. But what about herself? If her mother thought that soccer was hazardous, she might take Amanda off the team. An envelope full of newspaper articles about soccer's dangers might make her think about doing just that!

Eddie had been late to practice that morning. Could she have been busy shoving such an envelope through the Calers' mail slot?

Amanda shook her head. She didn't want to believe Eddie would do something like that. But the more she thought about it, the more it seemed to make perfect sense that Eddie was the culprit—and Amanda was her target.

Then she remembered something else. In

the rest room, Eddie had wondered if Amanda was going to be afraid of the ball after being hit. Then that night, someone had called the coach to ask for heading practice. Could the caller have been Eddie? Could she have hoped that Amanda would shy away from the ball whenever it came near her? If so, then she got her wish, because that's just what Amanda had done for most of the practice.

Amanda didn't sleep well that night. She had bad dreams about huge soccer balls falling from great heights.

When she woke up the next morning, her dreams still haunted her. She shuffled into the bathroom and splashed water on her face. Then she looked in the mirror—and almost didn't recognize the person who looked back at her.

I look scared! she thought. *I've never felt this way before a game!*

She stared at herself for a moment longer.

Her tense expression changed to a frown. *Being scared is just what Eddie wants. Well, I'm sorry, Eddie, but you're not going to get what you want today!*

She marched back into her room and pulled on her shorts and Soccer 'Cats T-shirt. Then she stormed downstairs into the kitchen — and ran smack into her mother, who dropped the envelope she was holding. Newspaper clippings fluttered to the floor.

"Well, well," Amanda muttered under her breath. "What have we here?"

Chapter 8

"Ah, I see you're ready for the game," Mrs. Caler observed as she stooped to pick up the clippings.

"Darned right!" Amanda replied hotly. "You're not going to try and stop me from playing, are you?"

Mrs. Caler looked up. "Why, no," she said with surprise.

"Because you know," Amanda went on as if her mother hadn't said anything, "you can't always believe everything you read."

Her mother arched an eyebrow. "And what is it you think I've been reading?"

Amanda pointed to the clippings. "You know what you've been reading."

"I see," said Mrs. Caler. "And you don't think I should believe what I've read in these articles?"

Amanda shook her head.

"Why not?"

"Because the person who sent you that stuff wants you to take me off the team!" Amanda blurted out.

Mrs. Caler stood up. "What!" she exclaimed.

"It's true," Amanda said. She grabbed a banana and a bagel and headed to the kitchen door. "I know it's not right to say something mean about someone. But this person has been mean to me, so why should I be nice to her?"

"Her?" Mrs. Caler repeated. "Are you *sure* —?"

"I'm sure," Amanda interrupted. "But I'm not going to let her get away with it." She slammed the door behind her.

Amanda arrived at the soccer field ready to show Eddie — and everyone else — that she was not about to give up her place on the Soccer 'Cats team. If that meant getting hit with the ball, then so be it!

The game against the Torpedoes started off quickly. The Torpedoes had won the coin toss, so they had possession first. With a flick of his foot, the center striker sent the ball to his right forward, who dribbled rapidly down the sideline.

Amanda was on him in a flash. She snaked her foot in, stole the ball, and rocketed a high kick to Stookie.

Stookie trapped the ball against his chest and let it drop to the ground. Then he started dribbling toward the Torpedoes' goal.

Torpedo fullbacks were on him in an in-

stant. But just as quickly, Stookie got rid of the ball by passing it to Lou on his left.

Amanda swooped in behind Lou, ready to counterattack anyone who stole the ball from him.

Someone did. A Torpedo halfback nabbed the ball when Lou lost control of his dribble. The halfback dribbled away from Lou and Amanda. He scanned the field and pulled his foot back for a kick.

Amanda charged in for the steal.

Blam! The Torpedo blasted the kick and sent it soaring right at Amanda's head.

Amanda didn't have time to think. She threw her arms up to protect herself.

Chapter 9

The ball ricocheted off Amanda's arms and bounced to the ground.

Phweet! The whistle blew. The ref signaled for a direct free kick.

Stookie ran up to help his teammates defend against the kick.

"Man," he growled to Amanda as the Torpedo sent the ball flying high into the air and into the 'Cats' territory. "Don't you know handling the ball with your hands or arms is a foul?"

Amanda reddened. "I do know that. I just—just—"

"You were just afraid," Stookie finished for her. "Just like Eddie said after practice yesterday."

Amanda stopped short. "Eddie said that, did she? And what else did she say?"

Stookie didn't have a chance to reply. The Torpedoes had taken a shot on goal, but Bucky Pinter had made the save. He cleared the ball with an enormous kick to the center of the field. Stookie and the rest of the forward line chased after it.

Amanda followed. She was so simmering mad at Eddie for talking behind her back that she didn't notice when a Torpedo forward stole the ball from Lou. Too late, she saw her dribble past.

"C'mon! Pay attention!" Lou called as he ran after the Torpedo.

Amanda spun around and gave chase. It was no use. The Torpedo had a head of steam. She made it to the goal before anyone could stop her. With a sharp kick, she launched the ball into the net.

The scoreboard now read Torpedoes 1, 'Cats 0.

"Rats!" grumbled Stookie. He shot Amanda a dirty look.

Amanda jogged slowly to her position.

"Pull yourself together," she muttered to herself.

But she couldn't. A bad night's sleep plus anger at Eddie added up to poor concentration on the field. Time and again Amanda missed making an easy tackle, fumbled her dribble, or misdirected a kick.

The Torpedoes seemed to realize that Amanda's side of the field was weak. They kept sending the ball to their right forward, who dodged around a flustered Amanda with ease. Each time it happened, Amanda became more frustrated.

The whistle blew, signaling an indirect free

kick. Amanda was about to move into position when she felt someone tap her on the shoulder. She turned to see Eddie smiling at her.

"I'm subbing in for you!" Eddie said.

Amanda couldn't stop herself. "Well, good for you!" she cried. Hot tears pricked her eyes. "You got just what you wanted, didn't you?" She ran off the field and straight to the rest room.

Chapter 10

Amanda sat on a chair inside the rest room, her face in her hands. She had never felt so miserable.

There was a light tap, then someone opened the door.

"Go away," Amanda said, not moving.

"I think I'd rather stay," came a voice. Amanda looked up to see her mother standing before her. Without another word, Mrs. Caler folded Amanda into her arms and hugged her.

"What are you doing here?" Amanda asked, her voice muffled against her mother's clothes.

"I came to watch you play, of course," her mother replied.

Amanda looked up. "But aren't you afraid you'll see me or someone else get hurt?"

Mrs. Caler smoothed Amanda's hair with her hand.

"Amanda," she said. "Who do you think sent those newspaper clippings to me?"

Amanda frowned. "It was Eddie," she said. Her face crumpled as she fought back new tears. "Eddie sent those clippings. She was hoping you'd take me off the team when you read that soccer was dangerous. She's been trying to make me afraid of being hit with the ball, too. That's why she called the coach to ask if we could practice heading the ball. Eddie wants to take over my position on the team."

"I do not!"

Amanda turned with surprise. There stood Eddie, hands on hips and eyes flashing.

"I called the coach about heading practice because I thought it would help you get *over* your fear of the ball," Eddie said.

"What?" Amanda was confused.

Eddie ran her fingers through her hair. "My mother always says that if you fall off a horse you should get right back on again. Otherwise you might never get on again because you'll be too afraid." She shrugged. "I thought if you were forced to head the ball over and over, you'd get over any fear you had."

"But yesterday, why did you tell Stookie I was afraid of the ball?"

Eddie rolled her eyes. "I didn't. Well, not exactly. He said something about how you weren't playing that well during the scrimmage, and I tried to explain to him what I thought was wrong."

Amanda had never felt so foolish in her life. Here she'd been thinking Eddie was out to get her, when all the time she'd been trying to help her!

"But what about the envelope with newspaper clippings? Who sent it?" she asked.

"I think I can answer that." Coach Bradley stood in the doorway. "I sent it. It's a standard package of information I like to give parents who are worried their little soccer players might get hurt. The articles talk about ways to make playing safe."

Mrs. Caler smiled at Amanda. "I was going to tell you that this morning, but you ran out the door so fast I didn't get a chance."

Amanda looked from her mother to the coach to Eddie. "I feel so stupid," she said.

"Not as stupid as I feel standing in the door of this rest room," Coach Bradley said with a laugh. "Which reminds me: Mrs. Caler, there's a phone call for you. Someone in the stands heard your pocketbook ringing and

51

answered your cell phone." He handed her the phone.

Mrs. Caler spoke into it. Then she turned white as a sheet. "It's Amelia! Someone in ballet class accidentally kicked her in the nose! Amanda, if you're all right, I really should go be with her."

Amanda said with a smile, "Gee, Mom, I thought ballerinas didn't get bloody noses."

Her mother flashed a smile back, then hurried away. The coach followed her, and Eddie turned to leave, too. Amanda stopped her.

"Eddie, I'm really sorry," Amanda said. "Can you forgive me?"

Eddie narrowed her eyes. "On one condition."

"Anything," Amanda said.

"That next time you'll talk to me before you jump to conclusions," Eddie replied. Amanda nodded.

"And one more thing," Eddie added.

"What?"

"Next time, don't be afraid to answer my question with the truth." She slung an arm around Amanda's shoulders. "And the truth is, I stink at halfback! I hope I never have to sub in for you again!"

"Don't worry," Amanda said, roping her arm around Eddie, "I'll make sure you don't have to! Now let's go win that game!"

And that's just what they did.